JO BUER

Between

A Gothic Novella

To all of my cheerleaders.
Thank you!

Between

"It won't be long now." The woman pinched the handle of the teacup as she brought it to her lips. She closed her eyes, savouring the first sip. A tui's haunting call flitted between the trees in the garden. Opening her eyes, the woman returned the cup to its saucer on the table. Her gaze fell upon the stretch of lawn before her, neatly cut and lush green, lined by untamed wildflowers. At the centre edge of the border, a small path trailed down the hill. To its left, two kowhai trees stood, their clusters of yellow flowers swaying in the breeze. To the right, a sturdy oak anchored itself in a bed of ivy. A stone carving, the size of a headstone, stood resolute amongst the first crawling tendrils of ivy. Into the stone's face a chiselled imaged of a strange dragon or taniwha unfurled amongst a teasing of moss.

Obscured from sight was a water feature. It nestled into the corner of the garden by the cobbled path leading from the driveway to the patio where they sat. A steady trickle of water fell from stone to stone until reaching the small pool below. If you listened really hard, on the very edges of the Eden, peeling back the veil, the distant sound of modern industrialism – of rubber on tar and the thrum of engines – took on a dreamlike quality.

A hand reached across the table, gently covering the woman's.

"Are you ready for this?" her companion asked, dark eyes searching her face.

For fifty years they had lived together, loved together, stood stoic against the pressures of their time. For near another fifty, they had lived *between*.

Their faces were autobiographies. Every fine line held a memory of laughter, every deeper etching, a lesson. Every discolouration and blemish paid an homage to time. Despite all the surprises life had brought, not once had they strayed from each other. For what was life without love, and death without companionship?

Ophelia turned her hand over, clasping Hilda's in her own, and gave it a small squeeze.

"Oh yes," she said. "I am always ready."

Hilda smiled, watching the light dance in Ophelia's eyes. In an instant, time disappeared. The air fizzed between them as the lines on their faces smoothed and the colour returned to their time-bleached hair. Each gazed with fondness upon the newly born face of their much younger lover.

Hilda touched Ophelia's cheek, stroking her soft, almost flawless, pale skin. A loose strand of auburn hair fell across her eyes, and Hilda brushed it aside. It never ceased to amaze her how time held no meaning here.

Ophelia moved her head ever so slightly, kissing Hilda's fingertips.

The air crackled and a flurry of confusion and flapping of wings burst from the garden and took to the sky. Far beyond, a screech of tyres and a crunch of metal reverberated.

"It's time." Ophelia stood up; Hilda's hand again clutched in her own. She smiled, her eyes unwilling to leave Hilda's.

Hilda nodded, her heart beating a little faster under her bodice. They had a job to do. A responsibility. The pleasure of being able to do it together never waned. Should everyone be as lucky as them.

They moved as one towards the carmine sculpted door that led inside. With her free hand, Hilda touched the Green Man's face, intricately carved amongst the fleur-de-lis plant tendrils and acorns adorning the door's surface. It had been some of her best work. She suspected the newcomer would think so too.

Ophelia turned the brass doorknob and together they entered. Their home. Their life. Their afterlife. The space between.

Rhea Harding dropped her phone and pulled hard on the steering wheel. The car swerved back onto the road, crossing the centre line. Rhea's heart jumped in her throat as she sought to correct the over-steer, the car weaving until it finally found its way onto the correct side of the road again.

"Fuck." She bit her lip hard to stop it quivering. White knuckled, she gripped the steering wheel hard and blinked back tears. That had been close. Too close. Yet her thought almost immediately went to her phone, likely stuck now in the thin gap between seat and middle console. The same place where the odd McDonald's fry would sometimes disappear.

Swallowing hard, Rhea gave an involuntary shudder. A glance in the mirrors gave some relief – no one had been around to see her mess up. Those signs berating *"Text and Die!"* weren't just for quips, then.

"Fuck," she muttered again, meaning it. She could have got herself killed. The road up Hosking's Peak was not only twisty but threatened demise with its sharp drop into a canyon and murky river below. A simple steel railing between road and death seemed a poor safety net.

She was so close. Three minutes if the GPS was to be believed, maybe a little longer. To settle her nerves, she reduced her speed. God, it would have sucked to die today. Today was D-Day. After a two-year hideous assault on her bank account, her figure (goddam comfort food), and mental health, today was the day she finally got to celebrate her divorce. There was no way she was giving her ex the satisfaction of learning she had been killed in a car accident before the ink had barely dried.

Oh, God. Another hideous thought struck her. She hadn't changed her emergency contact. He would still get the damn call. Him, or worse … his twenty-something grad student, the one he now shacked up with. What would stop her from being the first to take the call or to answer the door when the police turned up to report her dead?

Rhea slowed the car as the female GPS voice directed her up a road on the left. A white sign with an arrow signalled Cambre House. Rhea loosened her grip on the steering wheel. She was here. Mixed emotions fluttered in her chest. She had been looking forward to this for so long, just her and her best friend Sarah. A girl's weekend to celebrate her new start. But Sarah wouldn't be arriving until tomorrow. A kid emergency, apparently. Something about a trip to the ER, LEGO up the nose or something with the youngest. She'd have to check the rest of the text message when she officially stopped. It had been Sarah's message that had near killed her. She didn't know why she'd felt compelled to read it while navigating the tight turns, scrolling with one hand and driving with the other. She was an idiot. Only a moment had passed before the two passenger tyres were off the road completely, the nose of the car on a direct course for a tree which interrupted the metal railings protecting her from plummeting to her death. God, she had been lucky. How had she avoided a crash?

Before her, Cambre House rose above the trees lining the side of the drive. Gravel crunched under her tyres as she pulled into a small parking area alongside the house, its white weatherboards veiled with ivy. Two small windows on the second floor peeked out from nature's embrace.

Rhea had always loved the way ivy romanticised a place. It added a layer of mystique. Perfect for a place that proclaimed itself a respite for lost souls in search of themselves.

A fluttery feeling in the pit of her stomach diffused some of the shock from her near miss. After a moment of consideration, she pulled the car up along the fence line, facing away from the house, instead overlooking the rolling hills and low clouds of the countryside. She turned off the ignition and sat for a moment, a hand to her chest, breathing deep and steadying herself. Shock and excitement were a heady combination. She squeezed her eyes shut, then opened them, blinking hard. Everything seemed brighter here, more luminescent somehow.

Remembering her phone, she slipped her hand down the side of her seat, searching for the plastic case with her fingertips. When she came up with nothing, she scanned the small space the best she could in the limited light.

There. A little further back than she thought. Only with some deft manoeuvring and the use of both hands was she able to rescue it. Ew, a fry really was down there. She could just see it, out of reach, immortalised amongst dust bunnies.

She blew some fluff off her phone and ran the screen across her thigh before pressing the side button to turn it on. Navigating her way straight to her messages, she re-read Sarah's text – fully this time. She had the gist of it right. LEGO up the youngest's nose. Sarah would call later and do everything in her power to come in the morning.

Empathy didn't quell the disappointment. This had been Sarah's idea. She had been the one to convince Rhea that D-Day deserved its own special celebration. It made sense. People were so eager to celebrate birthdays and engagements, job promotions. Hell, even when a person died, there was a commemoration of sorts. It was even more important, Sarah had said, when the rite of passage signalled freedom from an abusive, cheating, low-life scum like her husband.

Sarah's original suggestion had been a drunken night of karaoke and pretending they were a decade-plus younger than they actually were. Rhea countered with a weekend retreat. She had the perfect place in mind, too. A lucky find squished between the pages of a random book left in the return bin at her library. A pamphlet promising a relaxing getaway. Something about it spoke to her. A century-old house nestled amongst native bush, with wildflower gardens, an intimate library, and vegetarian meals. Everything was overseen by two women referred to as the Sisters.

While it promised a realignment of spirit and soul and an assortment of New-Age woo-woo, all she wanted was a quiet place to spend time with her friend, enjoy the gardens, and maybe read a book or two, far, far, away from anything that reminded her of the last two years. The last decade, if she were honest. In the end, Sarah – who had originally rolled her eyes – had given in. Rhea suspected the promise of three full days without screaming kids had won her over. Sarah even paid for their booking. She probably needed this getaway as much as Rhea did.

Rhea typed up a reply letting her know she'd arrived safely. She'd share her near-death experience when she saw her next. She sent her best wishes for the LEGO retrieval and, as an afterthought, told her to drive safely tomorrow. Send.

"Unable to be delivered", popped up on her screen. Strange. It appeared there was no reception. She'd try again when she was settled into her room.

Stealing a glance in the rear-view mirror, Rhea ran a hand through her hair. The copper highlights looked great. Sarah had been right. She almost always was. If only Rhea had listened to her on the morning of her wedding, when she had questioned whether Rhea really wanted to go through with it. Her disapproval was written all over her face. It had upset Rhea at the time, but oh, what she wouldn't give to go back and change things.

Time to move on, she coaxed herself. This was the start of her new life. A new her. She'd be damned if she was going to let *him* spoil this moment too.

She collected her handbag from the floor of the passenger seat and, juggling her phone, opened the car door before stepping outside. Orbs danced in front of her as she blinked fast to allow her eyes to adjust to the glare. She stuffed her phone into the back pocket of her jeans, then hunted for her sunglasses. It must be the country light, she reckoned. Her eyes had acclimated to the urban haze.

With her bag slung over her shoulder, she moved around to the boot of the car to grab her duffel, taking a moment to relish stretching her limbs. Four and a half hours made for a long drive.

It took a bit of shuffling from hand to hand to get the balance right: handbag, duffel, and then fumbling with the key fob, waiting for the quick chirp that told her the car was locked.

A small sign on the side of the building showed the way to the reception, following a covered walkway.

Rhea practiced a smile in the hopes it might hide her nerves from whomever she met. Being here alone made her somewhat self-conscious. *I'm an independent woman*, she told herself, grimacing at how weak the words felt.

A door on the right stood open, leading into a cosy sitting area. Suspecting this was the entrance, Rhea stepped inside. A small table with an array of brochures and signup sheets for watercolour classes, chakra alignment, crystal healing, performance dance and other experiences said to align the spirit and soul – hocus-pocus, as Sarah called it – beckoned a future perusal. A framed painting of faceless wraiths dancing around a pentacle hung above the table. If it hadn't been for the pastel rainbow colours of the composition, which calmed any sense of menace, Rhea might have turned heel and left. The pentacle bordered on being a little too much. She was certainly curious to see what Sarah's reaction was going to be.

A couple of burgundy cushioned chairs sat on either side of the table. To the left, slightly out of view, was a staircase. To her right, another sign directed her down a hall towards the check-in desk. Rhea took heed, stopping at the counter that fronted a tiny office area. Within, a young woman with bobbed brown hair sat at a wooden desk, penning something in a ledger in front of her.

Rhea placed her duffel on the ground by her feet.

"Hi," she said, her voice a shade higher than natural, a symptom of her nerves.

The young woman, back to her, straightened her shoulders before facing Rhea, a large smile across her face. "Hello." She had an American drawl.

As she moved towards the reception counter where Rhea waited, Rhea observed her. Petite and pretty. She wore a pale-blue chiffon dress with a dark-blue floral pattern. It hung past her knees and had puffy three-quarter sleeves. Although a little old-fashioned in its design, it somehow suited her perfectly. In contrast, Rhea felt underdressed in faded jeans, ballet flats, and a mauve T-shirt.

"You must be Ms Harding," the young women said. "Welcome to Cambre House. I'm Natasha." She placed her hands, one on top of the other, on the counter.

"Nice to meet you," Rhea said in return, surprised Natasha had guessed her name. Surely, she wasn't the only guest checking in.

"We have you set up in room two—"

"There should be a second room, too, for my friend Sarah Harper," Rhea added. "There's been a bit of a family emergency, so she'll be arriving later. Likely in the morning."

"I'm sure you're right," Natasha said, her smile never faltering as one of her hands slid beneath the counter.

"We'll still pay for the room, of course." It hadn't been their fault Sarah would arrive a day late.

"Here we are. Your key," Natasha said, ignoring the point. She held out an antique-looking skeleton key, the like Rhea hadn't seen used outside of movies.

"Your room is up the stairs, second on the right." Natasha dropped the key into Rhea's open palm. "Dinner will be served in the dining hall at seven p.m. Do you want to see a list of some of our onsite activities?"

"Sure," Rhea replied slowly, her mind frantically searching for any mention in the brochure about there being a dining hall. That sounded fancier than she had expected. Did all the guests eat together, then? Her chest tightened. Socialising with strangers had not been on her agenda. Damn little kids sticking things up their noses. She'd be able to cope so much better if Sarah were here.

"Are there many people staying here at the moment?" Rhea asked, hoping her nerves would calm if there weren't many. No other cars had been in the car park although it would make sense if there was a second car park elsewhere. Where else would the staff park?

"Oh, you're our only out-of-town guest tonight." Natasha arched an eyebrow, a sparkle in her eye. "Our usuals will be here, of course, and I know Ophelia and Hilda are eager to meet with you."

Ophelia and Hilda. She couldn't place the names, yet it seemed she should know who they were. Rhea tried to recall what she'd read in the brochure, but she could no longer remember a lot. It was all a bit of a blur.

Natasha interrupted her thoughts. "The Sisters." She cocked her head. "Although, of course, they're not really sisters." Excitement lit her face as she bounced on the balls of her feet. "Cambre House. It's because of them any of this is here." She swung her arms out wide.

She obviously loves her work, Rhea thought.

"It's because of them *we're* here." Natasha's eyes narrowed in on Rhea, who shifted under her gaze.

"Of course," she said, not knowing how else to reply. She should have known about the Sisters, she berated herself.

Natasha, chattering on, pushed a couple of pamphlets of activities across the counter with Rhea only paying half attention.

Maybe the Sisters were mentioned when she made the

booking? She searched her memory. The names seemed familiar, didn't they? It's just … The realisation hit her. She couldn't actually remember making a booking. Her breath hitched. Natasha, oblivious, opened a brochure and pointed out a painting class she thought Rhea might be interested in.

Had she booked by email or by phone? Rhea wondered. A quick glance behind Natasha showed Rhea there was no sign of either. Neither a computer nor a laptop sat on the desk. No landline anywhere. Maybe a cell phone lay out of sight, she consoled herself. She was either more tired than she had supposed from the drive or else she was going mad. Neither thought was very comforting, but she couldn't ignore that there was a definite fogginess in her mind that she hadn't noticed before.

"Are you okay?" Natasha asked, reaching across the counter and covering Rhea's hand with her own. Her icy touch made Rhea want to recoil, but she stayed herself, thinking it rude.

"Oh, yes," Rhea replied quickly. "Just a bit tired from the drive, I guess."

Rhea gently pulled her hand out from under Natasha's and rubbed her forehead to stress the point. "Nothing a quick nap won't fix." She hoped Natasha believed her.

"Of course," Natasha cooed in sympathy. "Would you like some help taking your bags to your room?"

"Oh, no. I can manage." She was eager now just to get to her room. The sudden cloudiness in her mind bothered her. It wasn't normal. Oh, please don't let this be the start of a migraine, she prayed. She had heard of otherwise healthy people being plagued by migraines out of the blue. The thought was horrifying. But she was sure she'd packed some painkillers in case of an emergency. She could wash a couple down with a glass of water once she reached her room. Then maybe she would be able to think clearer.

"Thanks so much," Rhea added. "It was nice to meet you." She forced a smile, then bent down and picked up her bag.

When she stood upright, Natasha was watching her. Her hands rested one over the other demurely on the counter, her head tilted to the side.

A prickle of unease crawled across the back of Rhea's neck. The way Natasha was looking at her. She had seen that expression before. Rhea shifted her weight uncomfortably. It was pity. Unadulterated pity.

Rhea moved quickly back down the hall towards the entrance. Through the front sitting area, past the burgundy chairs, she rounded the corner to where she remembered seeing the staircase, spurred on by an unnatural urgency to get to her room.

She hadn't seen the man although how she had missed him, she would never know. But as it was, two strong hands grabbed her by the shoulders before she slammed into his chest.

Rhea squealed in surprise, coming to a sudden halt.

"Beg your pardon, ma'am," his silky voice interrupted. He still held her shoulders. Rhea's cheeks flooded with heat, made worse when her eyes travelled up from his chest to his face. She bit her tongue to avoid squealing again. The man who she had almost face-planted into was by far one of the most handsome men she had ever seen. He had a strong jawline with thin lips that quirked into a teasing smile, a boyishness amplified by the dimples on his cheeks. Yet when she looked harder, she suspected he was close to her age. What really made her legs quiver was his eyes, an almost supernatural kaleidoscopic green, the colour of which she had never seen before.

"Oh, I'm so sorry." Rhea stumbled back a step, her eyes darting around the room. He still held her fast, and she was all too aware of the warmth building beneath his hands. At this rate, she was going to burst into flames.

"No harm done," he said, dropping his arms to his sides, the timbre of his voice pulsing electricity through her veins. With her purse still slung over her shoulder, she moved her duffle bag in front of her, gripping the handle with both hands, a shield of sorts to put distance between them because surely nothing good could come from a man who looked like that. But oh, he really was something.

Mr Tall, Dark, Handsome, and Strong, if the grip of his hands had been anything to go by. His short, dark hair was longer at the front, with a fringe that was swept to the side. He wore beige slacks and a white shirt with the two top buttons undone. Something about him was both old-fashioned and timeless. Shifting her weight from foot to foot, she pretended to glance around the room, aware suddenly she had been staring. Pull yourself together, she willed herself.

"I'm Gabriel Owens," he said after a moment, holding out a hand.

Rhea placed her duffel on the ground in front of her and reciprocated with a firm grip. "Rhea Harding," she said, her voice pitching. She wasn't ready for the coolness of his touch, particularly as only moments before she's been burning up beneath his palms. Just like Natasha's, they were freezing. Unnaturally so. Yet somehow, she felt calmed by it. Like she'd been offered an iced facecloth during the clutches of a fever.

"It's a pleasure to meet you, Ms Harding," he said, maintaining a grip on her hand.

She willed him to let go before her legs buckled beneath her, while another part of her, asleep for far too long, was in anguish at the thought of him letting go. She wasn't sure who moved first, but all too soon the space between them widened, leaving a dull ache in its wake.

"You too," Rhea whispered her delayed response.

"Would you like a hand taking your bag to your room, Ms Harding?" Her Adonis nodded to the bag at her feet.

"Oh no, I'm sure I'll be fine. And I really am sorry. I should have been looking where I was going." The words rushed out, almost tripping over each other, as she tried to make sense of the assault on her senses. His touch, she was sure, was now etched permanently on her skin, and the scent of his aftershave was crumbling all attempts at composure, even as she avoided eye contact.

"No harm done. It is easy to do in this place."

Rhea eyed him quizzically.

"Things can sneak up on you quite unexpectedly," he rephrased, a hint of teasing in his voice.

Well. Didn't she now know it?

"Anyway, I insist." He took a step towards her, whisking her duffel up in one hand as if it were weightless. "Please. Lead the way, Ms Harding." He gestured to the staircase.

"Rhea," she corrected, allowing him to step aside for her to pass. "Please call me Rhea."

"Rhea," he repeated, as if savouring each syllable of her name with his tongue.

Stifling a shiver of pleasure at the sound, she placed a hand on the wooden railing of the staircase to steady herself, lest her legs really did give out. Amusement bubbled inside her on noticing a small sign on the wall asking guests to be mindful of their footing. She wasn't sure if the greater risk of her tumbling down the stairs was due to the short treads and high risers of the antique steps or her hyperawareness of the man right behind her.

She paused on reaching the first landing, instantly spellbound by the black-and-white photo hanging on the wall. Two old women stood side by side in a garden, their shoulders stooped and hair faded white. Filtered light from the branches of leaves above them cast shadows on their features. Their bodies, slightly turned into each other, hinted at a deep affection, even if their hands hadn't been clasped in one another's.

Close on her heel, Mr Owens's footsteps shook her from her reverie, and she flew up the final few steps off to her right.

On arriving at the top, Rhea fished the room key from her front pocket. She twisted it in her hand, weaving it between her fingers. Room two, she repeated to herself. It shouldn't be too hard to find; there were only a couple of doors on each wall of the narrow hallway before it took a sharp left turn. Almost immediately, a door with the number two carved into a small wooden plaque appeared beside her.

"This is it," she said, stopping short and turning to face Mr Owens. It surprised her to see him so close. Her nose almost touched his chest.

"Are you staying here too?" she whispered, her voice husky. He raised an eyebrow, and she blushed. "I mean, here, in Cambre House?"

What was wrong with her? It would be just her luck to be coming down with something. The flu maybe? Having travelled all this way to …

She struggled to finish the thought as prickles of unease settled across her nape again. Why was she here? She couldn't remember. She tried on different words. Was she here to rest? To visit someone? To celebrate something? Grieve something? Each thought hovered for the briefest of moments before disappearing. Nothing made sense.

She felt Mr Owen's eyes watching her. He hadn't answered her question. Maybe he wasn't a guest. Maybe he worked here.

He nodded towards the door, and with a start, Rhea shifted her attention back to the key in her hand. She tried her best to keep her hand from shaking as she lined up the key with the hole, inserted, and twisted. The doorknob turned, the door opening without even a whisper of a sound.

The room was small but cosy and warm. A four-posted bed stuck out from the wall, its cherry-brown wood sculpted into spirals. A quilt lay folded at the end of the soft purple bedspread. At the head of the bed rested embroidered cushions mixed with puffy cloudlike pillows, upon which a small bouquet of lavender wrapped in a large fern lay in welcome. On the wall above, hung another watercolour painting with faceless dancing wraiths. They appeared angelic with a halo of white light surrounding them. She was relieved to see there was no pentacle in sight. She'd seen enough scary movies to know a woman on her own in a strange place with a pentacle in her room was not an auspicious sign.

Soft, buttery, full length curtains framed a window view of the gardens below. A small desk and chair perched under the window. On the corner of the desk, a vase of fresh wildflowers mixed with more ferns sat beside a carafe of water with floating slices of orange and fresh mint leaves. A couple of glasses sat on a crocheted doily nearby.

On the wall opposite the bed, a low dresser with a wood-framed mirror stood, flanked on either side by a door. Her best assumption was one might be a wardrobe, the other, the entrance to the ensuite.

"It's beautiful." Rhea exhaled. She had never seen anything quite like it. It was homey and welcoming, like a warm embrace.

"Indeed," Mr Owen's said, startling her.

For a moment, she had forgotten he was there. She faced him, her heart fluttering at the intensity with which he was watching her.

"Where would you like me …?" He jiggled the bag in his hand

"Oh, of course!" Rhea said, willing away another flush of heat. "On the bed is fine. I'll unpack from there." She shifted out of his way to allow him space to move, but the room, being as small as it was, meant she still felt his arm brush past hers, setting all of her senses alight. She bit her lip, trying to steady her breath.

"You'll be joining us for dinner tonight, I hope," Mr Owens said, turning back to face her.

Unable to find the words, she gave a nod.

"Good," he said, his eyes crinkling at the corners and scouring hers once more.

"Thank you, Mr Owens," she said hurriedly, remembering her manners.

"Gabriel. And the pleasure has been all mine, Rhea," he said, drawing out her name. He gave her another quick nod, then winked before leaving.

Rhea closed the door behind him, listening to his receding footsteps before letting out her breath. Flopping beside her duffel on the bed, she sank into the mattress, where she lay for a moment, imagining she could still make out the lingering scent of his aftershave amongst the lavender and wildflowers.

"Gabriel," she whispered, paying attention to how his name felt on her lips.

God, was she in trouble.

Painkillers and a soak in the claw-footed bath did the trick. While the haziness in her mind hadn't disappeared, the tension in her shoulders had eased, and she was feeling less inclined to care about the things she couldn't remember. For the moment, at least, she was relaxed and happy.

Stepping out of the bath, she grabbed the nearest fluffy lemon towel and wrapped it around her. The sweet fragrance of the rose petal pot-pourri that had joined her in the bath clung to her skin. A small wooden bowl and scoop filled with the mixture had sat on a bench beside the tub. Rhea assumed it was meant for the bath, although now, listening to the strangled gurgling sounds, it worried her it might clog the drain. She should have scooped it out by hand before pulling the plug. But what was done was done.

Rhea stood in front of the small porcelain sink, above which an ornately framed mirror hung. Condensation had fogged its surface despite the open window above the bathtub. She wiped her hand over the glass until she could make out her own blurry appearance.

The skin under her eyes looked bruised. There were fine lines at the corners she hadn't remembered seeing before. Her cheekbones were a little more prominent, her face a little more drawn. How long had she felt this exhausted? Something inside told her it had been a while, yet the exact reasons behind her exhaustion remained wispy fragments of featureless memories. The most she could put together was that a man may have been involved, but beyond that, nothing. It was like a strange form of amnesia where certain memory banks were out of order. Maybe it was midlife malaise, she thought and gave a snort.

The mirror fogged up again until she too resembled a wraith, like one of those strange figures in the painting above her bed.

Snap out of it, Rhea, she admonished herself. She picked up her pile of discarded clothes from the floor and made her way back to the bedroom. The sun streamed in through the window, making her blink hard. It was still so very bright outside. She had thought it much later in the day. Hopefully, there would be time then to explore the gardens and snoop in the library before dinner. Fresh air and exercise would no doubt do her good.

After unzipping the duffel still perched on the end of the bed, she pulled out fresh undergarments along with a lacey shirt, opting to keep her jeans from earlier in the day. For a moment, she wondered if there was an expectation to dress up for dinner. She hoped not. She had always been about comfort. She'd thrown a couple of dresses into her bag on the off chance she might need them in an emergency. Dinner hardly felt like an emergency. Midlife malaise, she chided herself again.

Although ... hadn't Gabriel said he expected to see her for dinner? Oh jeez, Louise. Dating had not been on her radar, and now here she was feeling like a love-struck adolescent. Nope. She was better than that. She'd stick to her principles and not give her power away. Any guy worth his weight wouldn't care what she wore to dinner.

Then again, she reasoned, a quick splash of makeup never harmed anyone.

It was amazing what a touch of light foundation, a dab of mascara, and a swipe of lip gloss could do for a girl's confidence. Rhea used her towel this time to clear the condensation from the mirror. Much better, she thought, giving a small smile. She was definitely a pass.

The nagging feeling she was forgetting something of importance returned, but the more she tried to put her finger on it, the further the thought receded. Surely, if it had been that important, she'd remember whatever it was.

Fresh air. She definitely needed fresh air.

It took her a moment to locate where she had put the room key. On the desk by the window. Right next to her phone.

Her phone.

She picked it up, turning it over in her hand as a thought struggled to the forefront of her mind. Then for the briefest second, as if the Red Sea had parted, clarity hit. She should call Sarah. Sarah. Her best friend. Who was supposed to be with her. Here. Now.

Of course. Rhea needed to check in on her, see how her progeny was getting on, and make sure she was still going to join her in the morning. How had she forgotten? She had so much to tell her, not least, the handsome guest she was unwillingly crushing on.

Spurred on by an urgency that she might forget again, Rhea turned on her phone. It surprised her to see the long list of missed calls, all from Sarah. How had she not heard her phone ring? She hit the green receiver symbol to return the call. No ringing came on the other end. The call ended abruptly. She tried again. Same thing. It took a moment to realise there was no reception. No little bars signalling access to civilisation. Strange. Surely there was a cell tower around somewhere.

Her first mission on her walk then was to find somewhere with a signal. If she could call Sarah, maybe she could quash some of the guilt she was feeling for having forgotten her best friend altogether until now.

She locked up her room and made her way back along the

corridor to the staircase. She had that prickly feeling again. What kind of place didn't have cellular coverage?

She held the handrail as she made her way down the stairs. The narrow steps certainly made it trickier on the way down than up.

In fact, from what she'd seen so far, there was a distinct lack of any sort of technology at Cambre House. No television in the rooms, which, if she were honest, didn't bother her. But she also couldn't recall being offered a Wi-Fi password. And no obvious computer system set up at the front desk for reservations was a bit weird, wasn't it?

She hadn't come here for the technology, she reminded herself. Surely there would be a landline or radio in case of emergencies.

Get it together, Rhea, she reprimanded herself. What kind of person was she if being technology-free for a weekend gave her the jitters? She was here to relax and enjoy herself and ... there was another reason too.

Did it have something to do with Sarah? A celebration maybe? It was like grasping for water and watching it trickle between her fingers.

She continued down the stairs, feeling a hint of disappointment when she reached the bottom and there was no handsome stranger to bump into. It was almost eerie how quiet and devoid of life Cambre House now seemed to be.

Rhea took a moment to get her bearings. She could head back out through the lobby towards the car park and make her way around to the garden from the side, but surely there was another way. To her left was a tall, thin stained-glass window with crimson and violet roses and creeping green vines adorning the wall, beside which stood a dark wooden door with an old-fashioned deadlock. A portal to the outside world, she thought.

The door was unlocked. She couldn't explain why it would have seemed wrong somehow for her to have to unlock it herself, like she was leaving without permission. Had this been a hotel or something more urban, the risk of unlocking a closed door could mean setting off an alarm.

The door opened onto a patio. Two tables were laid out before her, one to her left and one to her right. Both were draped with white tablecloths with floral prints around their edges, the pattern matching the stained-glass window. The one on her left was rectangular. Wooden high-backed chairs surrounded it. A while porcelain bowl full of oranges and apples sat dead centre. A carafe of water, similar to the one in her room, sat next to several overturned glasses. This water, Rhea noticed, also held a few slices of orange and a sprinkle of mint leaves. Two of the walls around the table had built-in benches. Tropical flora themed bench cushions held square embroidered back cushions depicting trees in various seasons.

The walls above the built-in were vertical boards painted a lemony yellow. On the larger of the two walls, a colourful mosaic scene of two tui birds surrounded by lush vegetation stole the show. To Rhea's right, a smaller round table stood surrounded by more high-backs. In the centre of this table, a white platter held seedy crackers, a bunch of red grapes, and an assortment of cheeses. It was a picnic awaiting people to attend.

The patio's red cobbled floor extended beyond the overhang of the roof to create a path running in both directions along the sides of the house. Beyond the path, various plants and flowers almost entirely encircled a large lawn area. Rhea stepped out from under cover onto the path at the edge of the patio. The sun shone differently here. Rhea grabbed the sunglasses resting on her head and pulled them down to protect her eyes.

It really was beautiful here. The sweet scent of jasmine came from a vine woven around one of the patio's green beams. A gentle thrum of bees going about their business and a chorus of sweet birdsong was a pleasant reprieve from the uneasy silence she'd experienced only moments before inside.

Stepping out onto the lawn, she noticed what might be a path leading off through a break between two trees. Kowhai trees stood on the left, and a giant oak was on the right. Under the oak, a small outside table and chairs sat. A perfect spot to read a good book. The oak looked familiar though it took her a moment to place it. The photo on the landing in the stairwell. The two elderly women whose photo it was, could very well have been standing under this same tree. The tree seemed a little taller now and fuller, but it made sense.

With the fresh air clearing her head, she remembered the reason she'd come outside.

She pulled her phone from her back pocket, pressed the on button, and then went about holding it high in the air, searching, as she had seen in the movies, for a few bars of coverage.

Nothing.

She walked around the outskirts of the lawn, waving her arm slowly in the air as she did. Coverage had to exist somewhere. When she listened carefully, she was sure she heard the distant white noise of traffic in rush hour. Having completed one circuit of the lawn, she headed to the path leading downhill away from Cambre House. It was narrow, weaving past a small rose garden on the left, and becoming sheltered on either side by tall grasses, flaxes, and wildflowers.

Rhea followed the red pavers. Maybe the key to getting better reception was heading lower. While it didn't make sense in her mind, it was worth a try. There was a gentle gradient of wide tread steps, closer to landings of a sort. She paused on each one, checking again for those little bars of service. Still nothing.

The path twisted and turned some more, never putting into view its final destination. She hadn't gone far when her frustration took over. Despite sitting lower in the sky, the sun still beat down with a strange intensity. Suddenly Rhea was desperate for a drink. The orange-and-mint water waiting back on the patio called her name with fervour. Not finding cell coverage had made her agitated. Damn it. She needed to turn back. *You can survive a weekend without your freaking phone,* she reminded herself. Plus, if she really got desperate, there had to be a landline she could use.

Giving up, she stuffed her phone back in her pocket and headed back up to the house. *See?* She'd just squandered a perfectly lovely walk in nature because she'd been too focused on her phone.

Rhea took a deep breath, blowing it out slowly, annoyed with herself. She wanted to soak in the energy of this place. She couldn't deny there was something special about it. Holding her arm out to her side, she let her fingertips gently brush the flora beside her. She inhaled the wealth of scents, fresh, floral, and grassy all at once, like the best of spring and summer brought together. The knot between her shoulder blades loosened again.

On reaching the little rose garden, she paused. Someone stood there, a few metres away. The wide-brimmed hat obscured the woman's features. She had a trowel in her hand and was turning the soil amongst some of the rose bushes. Weeding, Rhea assumed on seeing a small tangle of weeds in a pile beside her.

The woman hadn't noticed her yet, and Rhea struggled with fleeting indecision and embarrassment. How long had the woman been there? Had Rhea walked past her on her way down without noticing her? Should she offer a cheerful hello, drawing attention to herself, or pretend she hadn't noticed her, and continue on her way?

"Did you find what you were looking for?" a rich voice interrupted her thoughts.

The woman slowly stood up to face her.

"Sorry?" Rhea said, for a moment not understanding the question.

"Did you find what you're looking for?" the woman asked again. "Most people who come here are searching for something." She pulled a gardening glove from one of her hands. With her free hand, she pulled off her hat and wiped the sweat from her forehead.

"Oh," Rhea said, a little confused. "I was looking for a cell signal. I can't seem to find one anywhere." She couldn't take her eyes off the woman, who had an indefinable presence. The woman was maybe a decade or two older than her, despite having a smooth and almost unlined face. She had a gardening apron wrapped around her middle, and two plaits of fiery auburn hair fell past her shoulders. It took Rhea a moment to realise the woman was watching her with a crease between her brow as if she hadn't understood Rhea's answer to her question.

"Do you work here?" Rhea asked, changing the subject and pointing to the garden tool in her hand.

"You could say so." The woman smiled.

Rhea shifted under her gaze. The silence lengthened between them.

"My name's Rhea," she said, in another attempt to make things a little less awkward.

"Oh yes. I make it my business to know all my guests," she said, stunning Rhea.

So this was one of the women who owned the place? "Well, it's a beautiful retreat, and these roses are gorgeous." Rhea let her eyes drift over the flower bed where cream, yellow, pink, red, and apricot roses bloomed. Her eyes fell on a large natural stone to the side of the flower bed. An engraved plaque was screwed to its front. A commemorative stone of some sort. She moved closer to study it when the woman spoke.

"My name is Ophelia," the woman said, her voice demanding Rhea's attention. "And, yes, this is a very special place." A Mona Lisa smile touched her lips. "It is not for everyone, but dare I say, those who find their way here are usually here for a reason. What is your reason, Rhea?"

Rhea swallowed hard, her throat even more parched. What she wouldn't give for a glass of water – and an out. This woman made her nervous. Put her on edge. It was as if she could see through to her soul, like she knew more about Rhea than Rhea did herself.

Clearing her throat, Rhea searched her mind for a reply. "I have a friend arriving tomorrow," she said. "This was her treat. A getaway and a bit of a celebration." She bit the inside of her cheek. God, she wished she hadn't said that. It was nice that her brain haze seemed to have cleared, but now that she remembered why she was here, she didn't really want to discuss it. Inevitably, the next question was going to be Ophelia asking what the celebration was for, and despite being a twenty-first century woman, she still cringed at the thought of telling a stranger she was celebrating her divorce.

Ophelia ignored the bait. "You look hot, my dear. The sun

around here can be a little otherworldly at times. Why don't you head on up and help yourself to a cold drink on the patio? There's a jug of water with glasses on the table – I'm sure you've seen."

She was dismissing her, Rhea mused. Possibly also reading her mind. She nodded her thanks. "It was lovely to meet you, Ophelia."

"I'm sure we'll see a lot more of each other," Ophelia said before pulling her hat back on and turning back to her roses.

Yup, she had been dismissed. Rhea smiled to herself.

The water was as delicious as she had anticipated, although it did little to quench her thirst. Rhea poured herself a second glass and took a perch on the built-in seating, gazing out over the garden and lawn. It really was enchanting. The sun was lowering further in the sky, brushing everything with a golden light that made the greens of the foliage even more green, if that were possible. She took a moment to appreciate the surrounding space too. When she reached the lawn, she realised the door she had come through was painted a vivid red colour. More than that, on closer inspection, she found it to be intricately carved. A Green Man's face, the pagan representation of the god of the forest, took centre place. Branches with leaves and acorns wove together to fill most of the remaining surface. Various birds were expertly hidden within the design. She could just as happily lose herself in admiring the door as she could listen to the birdsong or gaze at the beauty of the landscape around her.

She was pleased to get away from Ophelia. Everything she had said seemed to have a dual meaning Rhea couldn't quite decipher. The way she looked at her had made her nervous.

At some point, Ophelia would make her way back up to the house. Unless she wanted to risk another awkward round of small talk, Rhea needed to cut her idle daydreaming short. She gulped down the remnants of her glass, poured another to take with her, then headed inside.

A stark difference existed between the outside and inside of Cambre House. For one, it was significantly darker. It took her a moment for her eyes to adjust and to figure out where she might go next. It had always been her plan to explore the library while she was here. But where it was located, Rhea had no idea.

It surprised her how easy it was to find. Immediately to her left, an unmarked door called to her. It wasn't like her to just go around opening random doors in an unfamiliar place. What if she were to walk in on something awkward? Sarah, however, wouldn't have hesitated. She had always been the bolder one. But Sarah wasn't here, Rhea thought with a pang of sadness. So if she wanted to find the library, she would just have to take the risk.

She turned the doorknob slowly.

It was kismet, she thought, as the door swung open into what was obviously the library. It was even more darling than she had imagined. Smaller too, but she didn't mind, for it certainly made up for that in character. It was near impossible to take it all in. On the wall to her right stood a large open fireplace with an intricately carved wooden mantle, continuing the nature motif of leaves and branches holding it in place. The mantle held a large quartz crystal, a small vase with an assortment of dried flowers, and two clay bird ornaments. But it was above the mantel which most caught her eye. Another framed watercolour painting. This time there were six haunting, wraith like forms. Although they were again somewhat featureless, Rhea thought she could discern three women and three men. The six figures stood leaning into the centre of the circle, their hands meeting up high in the centre. Rhea stepped closer, as something below them caught her eye. It was another figure – she was sure of it – curled into a tight ball on the floor in the centre of the human cage. The colours of the painting were again all muted pastels: greens, yellows, lilacs, and pinks. Yet she shivered on looking at it. For all the beauty of the colours, a sadness dwelled there too, emanating, Rhea thought, from the figure in the middle. Was she trapped? Hurt? Why didn't she leave?

Something else bothered her about the paintings, all of them she'd seen thus far. Why did they all have to be faceless and ghost-like in their appearance? Shivering again, she took a step back. She hadn't come for the art, she reminded herself. She had come to peruse the books.

It still took a huge amount of willpower to tear her gaze away.

All but one wall was fitted floor to ceiling with built-in wooden bookcases overflowing with books, yet still they piled high on the floor. A window spanned the length of one wall. Floor-length, red-velvet curtains framed the garden view on either side. Beside the window, tall throne-like chairs stood stoic. Their dark wood was intricately carved, and they were similarly furnished with red velvet cushions. A table in the middle of the room held piles of books. There was space enough to place her glass amongst two piles, which she did in order to fully give herself over to the gifts of the surrounding shelves.

She started with the bookcase between the fireplace and the window. An icy breeze touched her skin despite the windows being closed. The collection of books was not at all what she had been expecting. Books on philosophy were mixed in with various religious texts and biographies of famous spiritual figures, from the Dalai Lama to the controversial spiritualist, Madame Blavatsky. Rhea moved around to one of the other walls. Trailing her fingers along the shelves, she scanned the titles on the spines. Not a single work of fiction existed in the library, or not that she noticed, anyway. There were books on healing with herbs and homeopathy, interspersed with more esoteric offerings – texts on the afterlife and mediumship. Yikes, Rhea thought, there were even a few texts on demonology. The giant coffee-table books on art history seemed less benign than they did in any other library. It was as if the little library were a gathering place for everything under the broad umbrella of spirituality, history, and art.

She rubbed her arms to quell the goosebumps rising there; then, she picked up the nearest book to her, to prove she had nothing to fear. The title read *Elementals of the Plant Kingdom*. She opened it to a random page and screamed. The book thudded to the floor as Rhea jumped backwards, her heart racing in her chest. A giant cockroach scuttled across the floor, disappearing through a crack in the floorboards.

Fuck. Rhea shook her hands, trying to dispel the feeling of little legs racing across her skin. God, if Sarah had been here, they would laugh about this. She was even more of a sceptic than Rhea. It would be just like her to tease Rhea that they'd stumbled upon a secret cult or that Cambre House was haunted. Somehow, that would suit its aesthetic.

But Sarah wasn't here. Rhea was alone. The thought sobered her. She was here alone, in a strange place, with some rather strange people if she were being honest. Not including Gabriel, of course.

She took a moment, letting her eyes wander over the small space again. Maybe this place *was* the headquarters for a cult or something because there was definitely something unsettling at play, even if she couldn't place it.

And her mind …

She could feel it; the fogginess was seeping in again, fuzzing out the edges of her thoughts. It took her a moment to remember what she had planned for the rest of the night. She slowly made her way back towards the door, scanning the room as she went, half-expecting something to jump out at her. She knew it was ridiculous. There was nowhere to hide in a space this small. Without meaning to, she paused once more in front of the mantel, her eyes bewitched again by the painting. Oh, yes, there was definitely a seventh figure. One not quite like the rest, cowering beneath the others. She had changed positions, though; Rhea was sure of it. She was kneeling, her hands covering her face, refusing to see the figures surrounding her.

Something tugged hard inside her chest, making Rhea choke back a sob. Her hand involuntarily rushed to cover her mouth in case someone was to hear.

The sudden squeak from the doorknob almost sent her flying across the room, and a squeal escaped.

His figure almost filled the door frame. With both relief and embarrassment, she stifled another sob.

"Rhea? Are you okay?" The deep timbre of his voice alone calmed her racing heart slightly.

"Y-yes," she stammered, her hand now clasped to her chest to steady it.

A small line formed between Gabriel's brows. He glanced around the room as if he were expecting to see someone else.

Then his gaze fell back onto her.

"I'm sorry," she said. "You startled me."

"Mmm," he replied. "What are you doing in here?"

His question caught her by surprise. "Oh, I'm sorry. Am I not supposed to be in here?" The words tumbled out now, in an anxious heap. "I thought this was the library. I saw it mentioned in the—"

He put his hand up, and she bit the inside of her lip to stop her torrent of words.

"First, you need to stop apologising. You've done nothing wrong." His eyes locked on hers. "And two, yes, of course you're allowed in here. All guests are, it's just …" He massaged his jawline as if he were choosing his words carefully. "It's almost dinner," he said, changing the subject. "Let me escort you to the dining room?"

His smile didn't reach his eyes, but she would have followed him anywhere to be out of that room.

Gabriel held the door open, gesturing for her to lead the way. How gentlemanly, she thought, stepping forward. But she couldn't help herself. She spared one more glance at the painting. She squinted. The scene had changed again. The wraiths were dancing, still in a circle, one hand each in the centre. Yet the central figure, the one on the ground, who only moments before had appeared so distressed, was missing. She wasn't there anymore. Or was she? It was so hard to tell now where the body of one figure met another; the colours blending until she could no longer tell them apart. Rhea rubbed her eyes. Damn the brain fog. What was wrong with her? Paintings didn't just change. Tears prickled, and she blinked hard to stop them from falling. With relief, she moved into the hallway again. She had no idea where to go from there. Gabriel would need to lead the way. She turned to him. He was fixated on the painting the same way she had been. She bit her lip to stop from asking what he was seeing. Did she even want to know? Her whole body trembled. She couldn't help it. She crossed her arms to stifle the tremors.

Slowly, as if he were being pulled from a trance, Gabriel's gaze moved back to her. This time, he didn't even try to cover up with a smile. Instead, he stepped through the door and closed it solidly behind him.

After a pause, he spoke. "It will all make sense eventually."

Confused, Rhea scoured his face for more. What would make sense eventually? She didn't understand.

A pained expression flitted across his face.

"Come on," he said, his tone changing again. "Food and a drink will do you good."

"My drink!" Rhea exclaimed, remembering she'd left her glass on the table amongst the books. Instinctively, she reached around him for the door handle. But his reflexes were faster, and his hand grabbed the doorknob first, stopping her.

"No," he said. "Leave it. Come on, they'll be waiting for us."

Before she could question who exactly "they" were, Gabriel's hand gently pressed on her lower back, guiding her away from the door. Despite the fear that had ricocheted through her body only seconds before, she relaxed into his touch. Warmth pooled in her abdomen and coursed through her limbs. Some rational part of her knew it wasn't even that his hand was warm. Far from it. Yet somehow the iciness of his fingertips seemed to alchemise into heat in her body, warming her from the inside out. Her cheeks flushed.

She let him steer her down the hallway, revelling in his closeness, anticipating how very jolting it was going to be when he finally stepped away. Whatever powers this man – this stranger – had, she was fast becoming locked under his spell.

Moving beyond the lobby through another small sitting area, Gabriel led her to the dining room. Cambre House, although compact, felt a bit like a maze where one room opened into another. It wouldn't take much to get lost.

Double doors opened to a rectangular room, not overly big but large enough for a long table in the middle: an exquisite slab of wood sealed in clear resin. Gabriel's hand still rested on Rhea's lower back, soothing her.

She hadn't expected everyone to be sharing one table for a meal, although who everyone was, she still wasn't sure. Would Natasha be joining them? Ophelia would, she was sure. And Gabriel. That left three placings unaccounted for.

In the centre of the table, a solid pillar candle with small purple flowers sealed in its wax sat upon a rainbow-coloured silk scarf. Its colours were so close to the painting in the library that her stomach flipped. Crystals and shells were scattered around it. A small handbell and a snuffer stood nearby. Her first thought was that it was a mini altar. Many people like to say a small prayer of thanks before eating, she reminded herself. Nothing to be anxious about.

She had been right; when Gabriel withdrew his hand from her lower back, a dull ache remained in its place. He moved around to the far side of the table where windows looked out on to a different garden. Another open fireplace sat behind the head of the table. To her relief, the paintings above were three small floral designs. Nothing ominous. Nothing haunting but for their pastel colours and their slight blurriness at their edges, like an image as one wakes from a dream.

"Come. Sit by me," Gabriel said, pulling out a chair.

"Oh, I should go change or something," she said, aware she was still in her comfort clothes. A dress would have been a better choice for the occasion.

"You're perfect as you are," Gabriel said.

The heat returned to her cheeks, and a light flickered in his eyes.

"No one here is fussed about that kind of thing."

She wasn't sure if he was just trying to be nice. He still wore his slacks and dress shirt. Damn, he really was handsome. She swallowed hard. Imagine what was under that shirt …

She glanced away, feeling another rush of heat. At the quirk of his mouth, Rhea wondered if he could read her thoughts.

She joined him around the other side of the table, allowing him to seat her and push her chair in.

"Water?" he asked, moving over to the sideboard where a carafe of water sat with glasses. "Or something a little harder?" he asked, opening the lower cupboards of the sideboard to showcase an extensive array of liquors and wines and their complementary glasses.

"Water's fine," she said without hesitating. The fogginess was still there on the periphery of her brain. The last thing she needed was a drunken haze or hangover to add to the mix.

He filled two glasses of water and placed them on the table, then pulled out a chair beside her and sat down.

She wasn't sure how any of this worked. Were there menus to choose from, or would food just be brought out? She tried to remember what she might have read from the brochure, but again, it seemed so hard to recall. In fact, she was struggling again to remember why she was even here. Didn't she have a life elsewhere?

As if sensing her turmoil, Gabriel took his hand gently in hers.

"It's okay," he said, giving it a gentle squeeze. "You're safe."

She looked up at him then. It was simultaneously a strange thing to say, but also the right thing. Because, even in her hazy state of mind, she was sure she wasn't imagining something was wrong beyond her momentary memory loss.

She wriggled in her chair, bumping against a small bulge in her back pocket. Her phone. She'd forgotten all about it. Letting go of Gabriel's hand, she pulled out her phone and turned it over in her hand. It felt so out of place somehow. Instinct had told her it was her phone before she'd even held it, yet she couldn't for the life of her determine why she had it with her. Had she been trying to call someone? Who exactly would she call? Gabriel was here. He was the only one she needed. Right?

"Here. Let me." He reached for the phone.

Without thinking, she gave it to him. Why wouldn't she? She had no use for it, and he always had her best interests in mind. All these years …

No! The thought brought her up abruptly, and she shook her head to make sense of everything. She hadn't known him for years. They'd only just met.

"How long have I been here?" she asked, her voice small, feeling ridiculous at the question.

He opened his mouth as if to say something, a hint of pity in his eyes.

"Oh wonderful! You found your way, then! And right on time." Natasha's American accent broke the spell. The air practically crackled around her as she entered the room with the energy often attributed to the carefreeness of youth. In her hands, she held a large wooden bowl of what looked like a rice salad.

"The others should be joining us shortly." She placed the bowl on the table.

"Would you like some help?" Gabriel offered, lifting himself from his chair.

"Oh, I can help too," Rhea said, shuffling in her seat. The last thing she wanted was to be left alone.

"No need at all, Ms Harding. You're a guest. Please stay where you are," Natasha was quick to answer.

A look passed between Natasha and Gabriel, and Rhea's stomach dropped.

"Gabriel, I think Maxwell's been searching for you in the lobby."

Gabriel turned to Rhea. "I won't be long." He slipped her phone into the pocket of his slacks.

They both nodded in her direction before exiting the room, leaving her alone.

Shakily, Rhea took another sip of water. She was at a complete loss for what else to do. She glanced around the room. There was nothing ominous about it, nothing that could account for her unease. Maybe it was just her aversion towards social occasions. Mingling with people she didn't know had always caused her lots of anxiety.

It was still light enough to see the gardens through the large French doors at the end of the room. Time itself seemed to move slower here, Rhea mused. The last of the sun's rays painted everything in a surreal glow, both haunting and beautiful. The garden, she realised, was a big draw for this place. She wondered if the reason she had come here had something to do with the gardens. Instinctively, she knew she'd never spent much time outdoors. She wasn't likely a gardener then, in her other life. But she did have a deep-seated appreciation for bird and plant life. Maybe that had been it. Maybe she had needed an escape from the real world, to rest and regroup, though she had no idea what would cause her to feel such a way.

Footsteps and voices in the other room brought her attention back. An old man with a balding head covered by a loose comb over entered the room. He was fully dressed in a suit and leaning heavily on an old-fashioned walking stick. Following him closely was Natasha. This time she carried a platter with an array of cooked veggies, seeded bread, and what looked like a small bowl of herb butter and olive oil.

"Oh, I see our guest has arrived," the old man said, focusing on Rhea. When he ambled around the table to where she sat, she hesitantly pushed her chair out and stood up. Despite his overall frail stature, the old man moved with surprising swiftness, and so it was with surprise too when he grabbed her hand in his, bringing it to his lips to plant a kiss. His touch was icy, causing goosebumps to rise on her arms. He dropped her hand, his eyes rising to hers, surprisingly youthful amongst a maze of wrinkles.

"Very new. Very new," he mused.

"Mr Hemmingway, I have you seated here," Natasha's voice rang out, breaking the spell. She had already arranged the platter on the table and was pulling out a chair on the other side of the table.

"This is Ms Harding," she said, introducing Rhea. "And Ms Harding, do not be put off by Mr Hemmingway here. He is really quite harmless." She gave a chuckle as the old man made his way back around to the other side of the table.

"Nice to meet you," Rhea said as Mr Hemmingway slid into a chair across from her. "Please, call me Rhea."

"Mr Hemmingway has been a fixture here for longer than I

can remember," Natasha teased. It was obvious she had great affection for the old man.

"That, my child," he said in an equally teasing tone, "is because I have been coming here since well before you were born." He leant across the table in Rhea's direction and whispered, "In fact, I was one of the first."

"Later, Mr Hemmingway. Save your stories for later," Natasha warned. "We don't want to overwhelm our guest. She hasn't met the Sisters yet. Unless—" She raised an eyebrow at Rhea.

Rhea shifted uneasily in her chair. "I don't think so …" Her brain refused to cooperate. She vaguely remembered meeting a woman in the garden earlier. Ophelia, was it? If she was one of the Sisters, she hadn't said so.

"Sisters? Are they still calling themselves that?" Mr Hemmingway's voice boomed. "How long are they going to continue that misnomer? Sisters. Pfft!"

"Here, have a drink." Natasha popped a crystal glass with a small amount of amber liquid at the bottom, in front of Mr Hemmingway, giving him a warning glare.

"I don't understand," Rhea said, in a small voice. "Are the Sisters the owners of Cambre House?"

Natasha and Mr Hemmingway eyed each other. Natasha's lips quivered as if she were about to giggle.

"All will be answered soon enough." She focused on fixing herself a drink, then pulled out a chair and took a seat beside Mr Hemmingway.

A flurry of activity erupted with Gabriel and a younger man entering the room, their arms laden with a tray each of food dishes. Rhea felt a wave of relief on seeing Gabriel. Natasha's face lit up in almost the same way on seeing the young man entering behind him.

The younger man seemed a little less sure of himself. Following Gabriel's example, he placed the dishes on the table around the centrepiece, and then, glancing awkwardly in Rhea's direction, he gave a small nod, before pulling out a chair beside Natasha. Gabriel moved around the table, taking his place beside Rhea.

"Maxwell," Natasha turned to the man beside her, "this is our new guest, Rhea. Rhea, this is Maxwell. He's like you: a recent acquisition of Cambre House."

"Hello," he mumbled in her direction.

What had Natasha meant? Confused, she looked in Gabriel's direction. How was she an acquisition? Gabriel focused on his drink, refusing to look at her.

"I'm just here for a couple of days," Rhea said. But Natasha knew that. She had taken the booking, hadn't she?

Natasha held her gaze and winked. "Of course you are," she said.

Rhea's spine stiffened.

Beside Natasha, Maxwell kept his eyes glued to the table. He appeared to be somewhere in his twenties, with shallow cheeks and dim-blue eyes. A sadness clung to him.

"Do you all live here?" Rhea asked, not sure where the question came from. She expected a grunt or a giggle but got neither.

"In a way," Natasha said. "We come and go as we're needed, but in many ways, yes, Cambre House is our home. The Sisters, of course, they live here, day in, day out—"

"—Never leaving," Mr Hemmingway finished.

The room fell quiet.

The sound of heels on floorboards drew Rhea's attention to the door again. As the two women entered, it was as if a collective breath were exhaled. Except for Rhea, who did the opposite. Instinctively, she knew these were the two Sisters, and, yes, Ophelia was indeed one of them.

Mr Hemmingway had said that calling themselves Sisters has been a misnomer. Both appeared to be in their fifties, carrying a strange youthfulness, particularly in the way they smiled and the glimmer in their eyes. But otherwise, they looked nothing alike.

Ophelia was the taller of the two by a good head. Whereas in the garden she had sported two pigtails down her back, she had changed now to a loose bun at her nape. Her very presence commanded attention. She had changed into a simple low-wasted green dress, almost 1920s in style.

The other was a softer looking woman, her eyes a magnetising brown. Her hair was a deeper brown with a hint of chestnut, a few silver strands framing her face. Her hair was styled similarly, and she'd chosen a pant-and-blouse combination with a tropical forest motif.

If Ophelia looked the more commanding of the two, the other woman seemed more welcoming. An aura of warmth radiated from her. Together, there was something alluring about them. But more than that – they were familiar.

Rhea willed her mind to think back to where she recognised them from. It was beyond having seen Ophelia in the gardens.

"Oh, it's lovely, Natasha," Ophelia said, taking her seat at the head of the table in front of the fireplace. The other woman walked around to the opposite end of the table to take her place in front of the French doors.

Natasha beamed. Nudging Maxwell with her elbow, she sent him a look that had him leaping from his spot at the table.

"Can I make anyone a drink?" His eyes shifted between the

faces at the table.

"No, thank you," Rhea and Gabriel said together.

"Ah, yes, a top up please. There's a gentleman," Mr Hemming-way said.

"Our usuals thank you, Maxwell," Ophelia answered, gazed across the table at her other half, who smiled an intimate smile. Rhea realised immediately why the Sisters was a misnomer. They shared a genuine love between the two of them. A level of affection that hinted at something she had seen before. But the thought slid from her mind too quickly to be grasped.

"It seems you've all met our lovely new guest," Ophelia said, surveying the room, as Maxwell set about pouring drinks at the sideboard. Gabriel snuck his hand under the table and clasped Rhea's hand, which again she was thankful for as she felt her heart beat a little unnaturally in her chest. She willed away a blush from having so many pairs of eyes on her.

"Ahem," a gentle voice came from the other end of the table. The other woman raised an eyebrow at Ophelia, then smiled mischievously at Rhea. "Since it looks like no one is going to officially introduce us, my name is Hilda Barrington, and as I've already heard so much about you, I assume you are Rhea Harding?"

Rhea nodded, smiling in agreement. "It's lovely to meet you, Ms Barrington," she said, noting how distinctly formal and old-fashioned it sounded.

"Oh no, you must call me Hilda. We all go by first names here," she said, throwing a teasing grin across the table at Mr Hemmingway, who missed it as he accepted another glass of liquor from Maxwell. "Except for Mr Hemmingway, but there always has to be *someone*."

Rhea, between the warmth in Hilda's eyes and the very real

feel of Gabriel's hand in her own, felt somewhat more at ease.

Maxwell moved around the table, leaving a glass of what Rhea assumed might be gin and tonic, with a twist of lemon in front of Ophelia. It came to Rhea that Ophelia looked very much like a gin and tonic sort of person. She would not have been at all surprised had she started sucking on the end of a pencil thin cigarette.

Hilda accepted a simple glass of water, and Rhea noticed Maxwell's hand shake a little as he set it down in front of her. As if sensing Rhea's eyes on him, he seized his hand with his other and turned back to the sideboard.

"This is such a beautiful place you have," Rhea said cautiously, looking from Hilda to Ophelia. It was Natasha who responded.

"Oh yes. But it's special in other ways too." Natasha winked at her again, leaving Rhea confused. Maxwell had fixed Natasha and himself a drink and took his place at the table again.

"It is certainly wonderful having another guest here with us. I do trust you're enjoying your stay?" Ophelia said, her voice strong. Although she said it to Rhea, her focus was on Gabriel.

So many secret conversations were going on beneath the looks that everyone kept sharing with each other. Rhea found it dizzying being on the outside. Undecided how to respond to Ophelia's query, she curved her lips into a small smile.

"Well, I don't know about the rest of you, but I'm starving," Gabriel said, lightening the atmosphere in doing so.

"Yes, yes, indeed!" My Hemmingway piped up. "Whose turn is it?"

Rhea looked around the table for clarification.

The weight of Maxwell's eyes came to rest on her, making her shift uneasily in her seat. His near-expressionless face unnerved her.

"Well, being it's Rhea's first day, I don't think it's fair to throw her in the spotlight so soon," Hilda said gently. "Natasha, since this lovely meal was your doing, why don't you do the honours?"

There was a gentle murmur and nodding of heads around the table, and Natasha bounced from her seat, beaming. Whatever *it* was, it was obviously something Natasha enjoyed.

"My pleasure," she drawled. Natasha bent over the table and lifted a corner of the silk fabric, pulling out a box of matches. Striking a match, she then leant forward and lit the centre candle. With a flick of her wrist, she extinguished the flame of the match, and dropped the match onto a scallop shell that was slightly blackened from obviously similar duties before. Then, picking up the small bell, she gave it a shake. It's tinkling tones sent pins and needles through Rhea's veins before disappearing.

Around her, everyone moved as one. Though the table had originally seemed so large, now it felt much smaller as a hand reached out for the hand beside it. Gabriel moved Rhea's hand clasped in his onto the top of the table, invoking a friendly smirk from Natasha.

Then all at once a stillness descended on the room, and those around her chanted together:

"Blessings be to those who came before,

And those who join us now

To share in these gifts from Mother Earth

That we may gain sustenance and strength

From the bounty before us.

May our eternal lives be blessed

By this humble harvest."

Every person at the table knew it, yet Rhea had never heard it before. It was not grace as she traditionally knew it and had half-expected it to be. The solemnity of the moment spoke volumes as to how well these people knew each other, and Rhea's isolation threatened to overwhelm her. What was she doing here?

Natasha released Maxwell's hand and rang the bell once more, which seemed to signal for everyone to drop hands. Which even Gabriel did, only adding to her loneliness.

"And with that," Natasha said to Rhea, "we eat." All at once, the table came alive. Maxwell shared platters around, while the others went about shovelling scoops of rice and vegetables onto their plates. From each direction, Rhea was offered food to add her plate. Diligently, she did. The food smelled wonderful, and although not naturally vegetarian, there was something to be said for the bright colours and aromas of the food before her.

From there, conversation flowed easily. It was Gabriel who filled Rhea in on who the surrounding people were. Often to friendly banter and small corrections.

Rhea learnt that Cambre House did indeed belong to Ophelia and Hilda, yet no one mentioned their nickname of the Sisters directly. Rhea could fill in the gaps. For some reason, Rhea had assumed the Sisters had been the original owners, which just wasn't possible. Ophelia and Hilda were much too young to have owned the house for the length of time hinted at. Rhea held back from asking about the previous owners or how old the place was. It seemed unimportant.

Observing the people around her, Rhea noticed how much they reminded her of a family. They knew each other well, that was for sure. Even Maxwell grew more animated and at ease while food was in front of him.

Rhea learnt Hilda was a talented carpenter and woodcarver. The dining table and the beautiful red door were made by Hilda's hands. Ophelia apparently had an unrivalled green thumb and was the artist behind many of the water-colour paintings around the place. On hearing this, Rhea stiffened, remembering how much the painting in the library had unnerved her. Asking if that was one of Ophelia's pieces was another question Rhea refused to broach. She wasn't sure she wanted to hear the answer.

Each person around the table had some sort of special gift. Natasha's culinary skills were apparent by the meal alone. Natasha was also praised for having a lovely singing voice. Maxwell, Natasha told her proudly, had in another life been an amazing musician. Why she phrased it like that, Rhea wasn't sure.

Whether it was the food or conversation, Rhea was beginning to enjoy herself. "Do you still play?" Rhea asked him.

He nodded slowly in response, then went back to eating.

Mr Hemmingway was a historian by nature, with an interest in philosophy. It was only Gabriel, who remained a bit of an enigma.

When Rhea asked how he came to Cambre House, he simply said that it had been more that it had come to him when there was nowhere else to go. Rhea scoured his eyes for a hint of what his words were hiding, but he glanced away and continued with the conversation around him.

"And you?" Natasha said. "Why are you here, Rhea?"

The table quietened for a moment as if everyone had gone back to holding their breath. Mr Hemmingway dropped a piece of cutlery onto his plate, and even Maxwell froze, his fork halfway to his mouth. Rhea let out a nervous giggle. Ophelia's eyes fixed on Natasha, her lips turned slightly downward. The other eyes around the table bounced between Natasha and Rhea. Rhea giggled again because, as hard as she tried, she really couldn't remember what had brought her here. Maybe she was drunk. That would explain a lot. She picked up her water glass and sniffed it. A little lemony and that was it.

"No one really knows why they end up here, Natasha," Hilda whispered.

Her head certainly seemed a little swimmy. Maybe she was drugged. Maybe that was it.

"Think about it, Rhea," Natasha said. A smile still plastered on her face and her focus unwavering. "This morning when you left your house and got in your car, what made you come here?"

Rhea tried to think back. Had she arrived only this morning? It somehow felt so much longer, like she had known these people for a very long time. Yet, she had a hazy memory of meeting Natasha that morning while checking in. She had discussed something with Natasha during the check in; she knew she had. She just couldn't recall what she had said.

"Enough, Natasha," Gabriel growled low beside her.

Natasha chuckled, lifted her glass to her lips, and took a sip. The energy around the table relaxed as people went back to eating, albeit in a slightly more subdued manner than before.

Yes, she had been drugged. Nothing else made sense. Suddenly the sound of people chewing, cutlery scraping on china, and the smell of food, was far, far too much. Bile rose in her chest as her stomach flip-flopped. She pressed her fingertips to her lips as a surprise wave of heat rose through her body and beads of sweat broke out around her hairline.

"Excuse me," she said, rising quickly from her chair, scraping its legs on the floorboards.

"Rhea?" Gabriel questioned, concern marring his features.

"I just ... I just need some fresh air ..."

And she did. The air in that room had become far too suffocating. She lunged for the French doors behind Hilda, making Hilda squeal in surprise.

"Ophelia?" Hilda cried out, across the table, as Rhea wrestled with the lock on the door.

From the corner of her eye, she saw the surprised faces of Mr Hemmingway and Maxwell following her. Natasha continued eating as if nothing were awry. Ophelia's jaw clenched, but she didn't move.

When the bolt in the door slid free, Rhea twisted the knob, just as she became aware Gabriel was by her side again. As the door opened, she lunged forward, almost falling onto the cobbled bricks outside. But Gabriel was there, his arms embracing her and stopping her from face planting.

The sun had well and truly set. The light from Cambre House made more shadows than seemed natural across the lawn.

Somehow, she unwound herself from Gabriel's arms and was able to make a dash towards the bushes before losing her stomach. Falling to her knees, her rolling stomach continued to fight against the resurfacing of memories she had somehow displaced. What was happening to her? And were they all in on it? Had they poisoned her? Was Gabriel part of it?

He was there, holding back her hair as she lost her guts again. As soon as she could, she weakly pushed him away. Whatever was happening to her, it wasn't right, and he *knew*. He was in on it.

"Rhea," he murmured, his voice sounding pained.

Wobbling, she made it back to her feet and attempted to bolt across the lawn. Her only intention was to get away, to go somewhere where she could think straight. Why was she here? And how had she arrived? Did she have a car? She still couldn't remember.

Feeling around the pockets of her jeans, she realised it didn't matter. If she had a car, the keys were not on her. Most likely they would be inside somewhere, and she really wasn't ready to go back in there.

All she wanted right at this moment was to get far, far away, leave this place behind. For her mind to be clear again.

The cool evening air bit at her bare arms, but she didn't care. She welcomed the coolness on her skin. A moon hung high in the sky, just peeking out from behind the branches of the oak tree. What did a red aura around a moon mean? she wondered. For there was definitely an unusual red hue to it.

She could just make out the path leading out of the garden ahead of her. Her body ached. A full-on ache, like the flu. Maybe that was it. She had the flu. She was delirious.

"Rhea," Gabriel's voice called out behind her.

Perhaps he did just want to help. She slowed down but refused to turn around.

The crisp air was clearing her mind. Not completely, but enough to make the fuzziness recede. On reaching the path, she noticed she could see a bit more. No longer obscured by the tree, the moon's near-full face lit the place up, more than she had expected.

Where was she going exactly? If she really was sick, the best place for her was probably back at the house. She turned around to glance at it, but a tall male figure blocked her view.

"Rhea." He placed his hands on her shoulders. "It's okay. You're safe." His words of comfort sounded like a plea.

The swimming in her head eased.

"Why am I here?" she whispered to him.

The edges of his mouth turned downwards, his eyes turned

glassy. "I'm so sorry," he whispered back. "None of us really know what brings us here, but if the Sisters are to be believed, there is always a greater reason, a greater purpose."

Rhea dug deep into her mind. If she could just remember something. Anything about before she got here. She back-tracked over what she could. She remembered this spot. She peered around. This was the rose garden where she had first stumbled across Ophelia. And there was the stone with the strange plaque. But why? Why had she been here in the first place? Her right hand twitched. Muscle memory. She had been holding something. Gabriel released her shoulders, and she turned in a circle, taking everything in.

That was right. The thought, though fleeting, came back strong and fast. She had had her phone with her. But who was she trying to call? She couldn't remember. If she had her phone, it would have the answers, she was sure of it.

"My phone," she said, turning to Gabriel. "Where is it?" She remembered now. He had taken it from her. No, she had given it to him. Why would she do that?

"There is no phone," he said.

"Yes, there is!" She stomped her foot. "I gave it to you," she accused.

When he shook his head, she let out a growl of frustration.

"There is no phone," he repeated softly.

"God!" she yelled, twisting away from him and kicking out at the nearest thing to her, the memorial rock.

A sharp twinge of pain shot through her ballet flat.

"Ow," she cried, tears filling her eyes. For the second time that night, she fell to her knees, this time dissolving into tears. He wasn't going to help her. Even Mr Handsome was going to lie, gaslight her. She was alone.

Sobs wracked her body.

She could still feel him standing behind her.

God, why wouldn't he just leave her alone? There had been a phone. She knew it, it was becoming clearer.

A bird call echoed through the night. A morepork, singing its mournful dirge. A banshee's call, the thought rose to mind. And she sniffled, calmed her sobs, and wiped her face with the back of her hand. She was stronger than this. Her foot still throbbed beneath her. It didn't matter. Nothing did, she realised.

The skin on her nape prickled. She could feel everyone standing behind Gabriel, their eyes like needles against her. Had they all come out to be entertained by the broken woman crying in the garden? Were their lives really so pathetic that this was how they got their kicks?

Well, fuck them. She wasn't going to just sit here wallowing like a baby. She wouldn't allow them the satisfaction. She would push past them, get to the house, find her phone, her car keys if she had them, and get out of this place. They could all go fuck themselves. There would be no five-star TripAdvisor review from her.

Her mind had cleared significantly. Like her anger had burnt off the remnants of whatever drugs they had given her. Surely that's what this whole sorry business had been. With a sniff, she wiped her eyes one final time, steeling herself to stand up and face her tormentors.

Instead, the first thing her eyes focused on was the stone before her and the words carved into its face plate.

"May those for whom life was hard
Be warmed by the love of souls
Whom draw near to you
And embrace you

Even in your darkness
So that you too may know
The kindness of eternity.
In this garden, the ashes of the following have been laid with loving hands."

Rhea's eyes blurred at the list of names and dates beneath.

"No," she mouthed, her breath stolen from her.

Strong hands lifted her to her feet, and as he turned her to face him, she saw them as she knew she would. Not a sign of malice on any face. Small smiles. Flickers of pity. And glimpses of understanding she had never seen before. Gabriel drew her to him, holding her to his chest, and she let him. She no longer noticed the coolness of his touch, instead, she felt warm and safe in a way she hadn't before. She caught the scent of his cologne and buried her face further into his chest, listening for the sound of his heart that beat despite all odds.

"You're where you belong," he whispered before kissing the top of her head.

And from that moment, she believed it.

Ophelia and Hilda sat sipping their tea, watching over their domain. All had turned out well. As best as it could, at least.

As always, it was another brilliant, sunny day. Tui sang their melodies, fantails fluttered from limb to limb in the oak tree across the lawn.

They never knew in advance details of who would be drawn to them, but they had learnt over time to recognise the ripple in the air when some lost soul was to arrive. They did what they could the best way they knew how. Both had always believed every soul had a reason for coming. It was their job, they decided, to help them adjust. Find out for themselves who they were. They would be the gentle presence in the background waiting to help them heal once they were ready to accept what had happened. Some stayed on. Gabriel had done so. He first checked in in 1938. It had been much different back then. For one, there had been no need for a glamour of any sort. Both Ophelia and Hilda had been much younger then – yet old enough to garner respect. And both, at the time, had stood with both feet in the living. They were old women when they passed, only days between them, Hilda in her bed, and Ophelia here, doing much as she was doing now.

Cambre House had always felt like home, but more than that, it was special. To the people in the town, the two maverick women living in the strange cottage on Hosking's Peak were sisters. At the time, it seemed easier to swallow than the truth. There had always been some who feared them and wished to have as little to do with them as possible. And that had worked out perfectly because it meant that only those who needed their services sought them out.

Cambre House, with them at the helm, had gone through many iterations. It had been an artists' retreat and a school for the esoteric. It had also been a simple bed-and-breakfast, an escape from the normal day to day. A retreat for lost souls even then, they decided.

With the support of their friends and a small inheritance left to Hilda, Hilda and Ophelia had acquired Cambre House and made it their own. For many years, it served as a gathering house for friends with an interest in philosophy, natural healing, and, yes, occultism. A place for those who wanted to explore the unknown. There had always been regulars, just as there had always been guests. Mr Hemmingway had been with them almost from the beginning. He was a historian on paper, but come Wednesday nights, he would lead a group in mediumship. In a way, it had prepared them perfectly for their present life.

But Gabriel … They had all been surprised when he arrived. He was not their usual sort of visitor. He showed no interest in mediumship or the arts. He was certainly no conduit for communicating with the dead, Mr Hemmingway had proclaimed. Gabriel had arrived with little interest in anything, if they were honest. So they should have known. Even alive, he had been a lost soul. He wore his grief like an impenetrable cloak around him. As one would expect, having lost his wife and two young children in a house fire only six months before.

They didn't learn of his family's deaths until later, of course. After the police had done their inquiries and his body had been removed from Cambre House to lie unclaimed in the local mortuary.

It had been Ophelia's plan. For as hardened as she sometimes seemed, the idea of such a handsome man being so easily forgotten tugged too strongly to be ignored. It had taken many bribes and calling in of favours, but Ophelia got her way. As she always did. With no living family to claim him, they released his body to her.

He had been the first. His ashes scattered amongst the roses. It had made sense since he had chosen this place, Cambre House, to end his life. He never said why he chose their place. Likely he didn't know. But like many who came later, he had felt the unexplainable pull. Not many stayed. Some visited for a while of course, but typically would leave when healed and ready.

Others, like Mr Hemmingway, hadn't ever shown any sign of leaving. Ophelia and Hilda could understand that. Who would want to leave such a beautiful place? Gabriel, it seemed, had come into his own since his passing. A mentor for those who struggled a little more than others. Like Maxwell, who was one of their newer guests and still finding his feet.

Ophelia and Hilda had never had a choice. It was their purpose. They had a duty of care. While alive they had opened their arms in welcome of all who came knocking at their door. It seemed only right to continue to do so in the afterlife as well.

Yet even in this in-between, Hilda and Ophelia had noticed a shadow cross Gabriel's features. It kept them up at night sometimes, lying in bed, discussing what they could do to help such a gentle soul.

They had known someone was coming. It was announced in the slight tremor in the tui's call, a change in the air. They had all become accustomed to the forewarning. It was always a little more bittersweet when it was someone so young, someone so reluctant to accept what was. In some ways, when they learnt Rhea's back story, it made sense she'd found her way to them. And on seeing her and Gabriel together, they couldn't help but believe a bigger hand had orchestrated things.

A year to the day, her friend had come. Ophelia and Hilda had watched her from their usual spots. They heard the car before they saw it. People didn't often come up here anymore. Sometimes young teens would make the trip to use it as a make-out spot or to try to scare each other about the haunted house on the hill. Cambre House was part history, part mythology. Some believed it was a hotspot for paranormal activity; others believed the Sisters were witches or the leaders of a cult that used the house as headquarters.

They had all been wrong. They preferred to think of themselves as scientists, endeavouring to learn about the human spirit through the great minds and works of those who came before.

Both the voyeurs and sightseers were harmless enough and easy to ignore. But this woman, they noticed right away, was neither. Her straight blonde hair was tied back in a messy mum bun. Dark circles shadowed reddened eyes, and it was obvious she had been crying for some time. She had a tote slung over her shoulder and carried a single yellow rose in one hand. Ophelia and Hilda watched with curiosity, knowing that what she was seeing was so much different from what they saw before them.

She walked up the path around the front of the house, where red cobbled bricks once led. Now the faded bricks were overgrown with weeds having forced their way between them. Very little remnants of the water feature remained. The gardens and lawn, which had been unkept for years, had fallen into disarray. As had the house. Now boarded up over the windows and doors in a poor attempt by the local council to keep out the riffraff. Graffiti coloured the peeling weather boards on the side of the house.

The woman's eyes were wide. It wasn't what she expected. It couldn't have been.

"It's Sarah," a voice behind them said. Rhea stepped through the red door. For them, it was still as vibrant as it had always been. In the other woman's world, sheets of plywood had replaced it many years prior, as some thief had thought to take off with it.

"Water?" Hilda asked, holding out the carafe as Ophelia pushed a glass towards her. They didn't bother with their glamour anymore. They didn't need to. Rhea had surprised them by how fast she had adjusted in the end. It would have been too much if she'd recognised them in the picture on the stairwell right away; better to be the thirty-year-younger versions of themselves and allow her to piece it together as she was ready.

In the end, the memorial stone had done it for them. There were names she would never have recognised, as those people had moved on, but four of them would have stood out. The first being a Mr Gabriel Owens, and if she sifted through the other names, she would have seen a Mr Arthur Hemmingway, and at the bottom, a Ms Hilda Barrington and Ms Ophelia Youngwood. Natasha's and Maxwell's were not included. Like Rhea, neither had died on site, so their ashes weren't here.

Rhea shook her head, but as Ophelia tapped the seat beside her, Rhea plopped herself down.

"She can't see us, can she?" Her voice held a slight tremble.

"No, my dear," Ophelia said, placing her cup of tea on the saucer before her. She reached an arm around her shoulder, pulling her close.

Hilda smiled at her and Rhea rested her head on Ophelia's shoulder.

"Does it get easier?"

"Oh yes, it does. In the meantime, you have us. Think of this as a rest stop until you're ready to continue on."

"But you two never did," Rhea said, and Hilda and Ophelia exchanged a glance.

"No, we didn't," Hilda said softly with no other explanation.

Sarah looked around her, her hand to her mouth, trying to take in the incomprehensible. Rhea had shown her the brochure; she'd seen it with her own eyes. And Rhea had made the booking. She had said she had. She'd even used Sarah's card. Sarah had insisted. It was going to be her treat. A celebration of D-Day, the day her divorce was officially finalised, and she was free of the bastard. So what had happened then? How was it that this was supposed to be the retreat?

Sarah rummaged in her bag and pulled out her phone. Full

coverage. She typed the location into the maps app. This was the address, all right. It made no sense.

Yet she'd seen the wreckage for herself. Not two hundred metres down the road from here. The road didn't lead anywhere else.

It had been one of the police officers who had called. He had been new on the job and forgot to follow protocol. She later learnt it had earned him a stern reprimand. Instead of calling next of kin, he had called her, as hers had been the last message on the phone they found in the car.

Sarah had driven up right away. She had argued with her husband about it. There was nothing she could do, he reminded her. Dead on impact. But it didn't matter. All that mattered was being there for her friend. Unless she saw for herself, she would never believe it. Her best friend, for near twenty years. This was supposed to be the beginning of a new chapter, not the end. It made zero sense.

Tears ran freely down Sarah's face as she turned around, scouring her surroundings. "I'm so sorry, Rhea." A sob broke free.

Rhea sat upright. "Maybe she knows I'm here. Maybe Sarah will be different."

Her eyes flitted from Ophelia to Hilda. Hilda shook her head.

She had to try. Slipping out from under Ophelia's arm, she ran to her friend. Neither one of them tried to stop her.

"I'm here, Sarah. I'm okay." She tried, tried to make her hear, but Sarah just cried harder, her hands over her eyes, her body wracked with tears.

"It's all my fault," she said.

"No," Rhea argued back. "How could it be?"

"It's all my fault," she said again. "They thought you might have been on your phone, and I … I was the last one …" Another loud sob.

Rhea tried reaching out to her. All she wanted was to put her arms around her, let her know she was okay. In fact, in some ways, things were so much better. Oh, Sarah would have loved Gabriel.

She reached her hands out for Sarah's shoulders, just as Gabriel had done for her. With a shudder, Sarah rubbed her arms, as if chilled.

"How could this happen?" Sarah whispered. "There's nothing here."

Rhea looked back at Ophelia and Hilda in desperation. Surely, they knew a way to communicate with the living, since they'd had such a special knack of communicating with the dead when they were alive. Surely …

She just needed Sarah to know she was there. She was okay. And it hadn't been her fault. There would never be a way to explain Cambre House. Living or not. She still couldn't get her head around it.

With a sniff, Sarah seemed to pull herself together for a moment.

"I just … I wanted to tell you … Oh, God, this is stupid." Sarah shook herself and pressed her hand to her forehead, massaging the spot above her eyes.

"I don't even know if you're here," her voice pitched. "Look at this place. How could anyone think you'd be here?" She peered around again. Everything was so overgrown. Forgotten. Left to rot. Yet she'd heard the rumours all the same when she'd done her research and found out Cambre House had ceased to exist a near forty years before. Sure, the claims had bordered on lunacy. Talk of lost souls and hauntings and such. But there had also been a mention about Hosking's Peak being a conduit between worlds. Something to do with ley lines. Never before would she have believed such a thing. At any other time, she and Rhea would have made fun of the aluminium-foil-hat-wearing weirdos.

But then, Rhea had chosen this place. It had seemed unusual even when Rhea had first shown her the pamphlet. Sarah had proposed a big drunken party at the local with maybe a hired karaoke system, but Rhea had put her foot down. In some ways, it had made sense. She had never been comfortable being the centre of attention and having a big fuss made about her.

So maybe, just maybe, there was a chance that she was here. Somewhere. Hopefully, in a nicer version of where Sarah was presently standing.

"Rhea?" Sarah whispered. "If you are here. Somewhere. Listening. I have news. I thought it important you knew." She paused for a moment, sucking in a big breath. "The bastard's been arrested. Domestic abuse. He landed her in hospital. Turns out her father is a big shot lawyer. All this time, it had been going on. You weren't the only one he laid a hand on. But you ... you got out." Sarah choked back a sob. "You tried to tell her. He broke her eye socket." Fresh tears streamed down Sarah's cheeks.

"He's going to jail, Rhea. You're safe." Sarah giggled amongst a sob.

But Rhea knew what she meant. For two years that man had harassed her, leaving her too scared at times to even pick up her phone. Not to mention the ten years prior of living in fear, being beaten physically and emotionally, being gaslit like it was all in her head, and threatened over and over again. If it hadn't been for Sarah, she may never had made it out alive. She owed her friend her life. As D-Day approached, she had been scared he might come hunting for her, for old time's sake. It had been part of the reason she had been so intent on getting away, somewhere where he'd never think to look for her. The irony was that now she really was safe.

Tears rolled freely down Rhea's cheeks. She wished her friend knew just how grateful she had been, still was.

Sarah sniffed again and wiped her face with the back of her hand. She turned to face the house and Rhea followed her gaze.

She had an audience. They had all joined the Sisters. Maxwell and Natasha stood side by side in front of the stained-glass window. Natasha's head rested on Maxwell's shoulder, and even from this distance, Rhea could swear, Natasha's eyes looked a little more red than usual. Mr Hemmingway had taken a perch beside Hilda. He leant forward, his hands clasped over the top of his walking stick, which stood between his knees. And there, by the red door, stood Gabriel. His head tilted to one side, watching her. Rhea felt another burst of warmth inside her. Yes, she was safe.

Sarah moved towards them, and for a moment, beyond all hope, Rhea wondered if somehow she could see them or knew they were there. Side by side they walked. In reaching the patio, Sarah paused, bringing the rose to her lips. When she gave it a small kiss, Rhea wiped another rogue tear. Bending down, Sarah placed the rose against the now-faded pillar, then slowly stood up again.

"Rest in peace, my friend." Sarah turned on her heel, then took off in an almost-run back where she had come. Rhea wanted to follow her. God, her heart ached, but she stayed herself. She was home now.

The car left, winding down the drive.

"Thank you," Rhea whispered, before turning around to face her new family. They waited for her with open arms. Even Mr Hemmingway, Ophelia, and Hilda had moved from their seats to encircle her and bring her into their embrace. In a way, D-Day had brought her a new start. Happy death day to me, she thought.

Free eBook!

Thank you for purchasing *Between*. I hope you have enjoyed it.
If you would like to be updated about my other books and
future publications, be sure to join my mailing list at
https://BookHip.com/PBVBNSV.
By doing so, you'll be the first to learn of new releases and
special offers, and get a behind-the-scenes glimpse of my life
as an author.
And when you sign up to my mailing list, I'll send you a copy of
my short story collection, *Between the Shadows* for **free!**

Enjoy this book?
You can make a big difference to keep this writer writing!

Reviews are an author's secret weapon.
Honest reviews of my books help bring them to the attention
of other readers and allow me to promote them to a bigger
audience.
In turn, this opens many more doors for me to keep writing.
If you've enjoyed this book, I would be super grateful if you
could share the love and leave a review on Goodreads or on
the storefront you've purchased this from. And remember to
tell your friends where they can find my books too.
Thank you so much!
Jo xx

About the Author

Jo Buer is a gothic suspense and paranormal cozy author living in New Zealand. She is a sucker for the supernatural, time travel, and all things woo-woo. From an early age she came to realise that sometimes truth *is* stranger than fiction.

She lives in an ordinary house in an ordinary town with her husband and feline familiars, Atlas, Gaia, Zeus, and Hades. When not doting on her cats, devouring self-help books or gorging on chocolate, she writes slightly dark, sometimes scary, often ghostly stories with a smattering of romance.

Jo is also the host of the *Alchemy for Authors* podcast - a podcast to transform and supercharge your writing life.

You can connect with me on:

- https://jobuer.com
- https://www.facebook.com/jobuerauthor
- https://www.instagram.com/jobuerauthor

Subscribe to my newsletter:

- https://bookhip.com/PBVBNSV

Also by Jo Buer

Unspoken Truths
How far will one small town go to bury a haunting truth?

1939

Gwendolyn Davies is determined to make it on her own. In the sleepy little village of Te Tapu, she accepts a teaching position and finds love with a local farmer. Yet, behind the closed doors of the boarding house where she resides, terror reigns and secrets stack up.

Tortured. Imprisoned. Threatened.

Gwen's only hope to survive is to risk her love, job and reputation, and escape before the secret she carries destroys them all.

Present Day

Riley Cooper is thrilled to win a teaching position at Te Tapu School until she learns of the town's dark history.

An unsolved murder.

A mystery Te Tapu is eager to bury.

Unnerved by the discovery, Riley sets out to uncover the secrets others would kill to keep hidden. The voices of the dead refuse to be silenced, leaving Riley with an unforgiving choice.

What is she willing to pay to bring the truth to light? Her life… or her sanity?

Journey into the gothic suspense found in Te Tapu, and discover what *Unspoken Truths* are buried there!

Buy it here today! https://books2read.com/unspokentruths

Rest Easy Resort
A cursed resort and unsettled ghosts will put one relationship to the ultimate test.

Hannah O'Connor wants to enjoy her honeymoon at the newly revived Rest Easy Resort with her true love by her side. Instead, her new husband is spending every moment on his phone, wrapped up in business calls and oblivious to the darkness closing in.

Hannah fills her time exploring the resort and inadvertently awakens an ancient curse that swirls and lashes in an ominous threat against everyone in its wake. Caught in a disorientating slip through time, Hannah finds herself faced with an impossible choice between love… and death.

Lives are in jeopardy. Marital bliss threatened by the hauntingly surreal. Will Hannah make the ultimate sacrifice to save those she loves?

Rest Easy Resort is the gripping debut novel of Jo Buer.

Purchase your copy of this haunting, gothic love story here: https://books2read.com/resteasyresort

Voices
Poignant, haunting, and deliciously dark.

Grab a blanket, hot drink, and maybe some tissues, and settle in for five compelling short stories by gothic suspense author, Jo Buer, including:

VOICES
Everything that dies comes back... someday.
While reconnecting with old friends, a mysterious voice and chilling song force a woman to confront her tragic past.

DEWEY DECIMALS
Tick, tick, tick. The red hand tiptoes round the face. Six o'clock. Time to begin.
A man with sinister intentions watches a librarian go about her tasks.

RABBIT SKIN
If you can't see them, they can't see you...
A young girl tries to make sense of her grandmother's death, and her grandpa's actions thereafter.

THE WALNUT TREE
Something nags at you. Something snarls and snaps and nips at your insides, making you pause...
A teenage girl comes home from school to find that something unsettling has changed in her parents' demeanours.

RUATAPU RIVER
The river remembers us as we remember it: the canoeing, the swimming, the paddling... It even remembers the drowning.
But how much is memory, and how much is imagination? And can intuition really precede death?

Voices is Jo Buer's second collection of short stories. If you

enjoy thrilling escapades into the many facets of grief and uncovering beauty in darkness, then you'll love this new anthology.

Poignant, haunting, and deliciously dark. Pick up *Voices* today! https://books2read.com/jobuervoices

Between the Shadows
A man waits in the shadows watching his lover with someone else.

A young girl must say goodbye to the only friend she has – a friend no one else can see.

A boy writhes in agony in his hospital bed as his sister tries to calm him with a story.

A mother must learn to let go of the child she has already lost.

Between the Shadows **is an eclectic collection of poignant and haunting tales about grief. If you like stories that fill the senses with ghostly interludes and meditations on life and death then you'll love Jo Buer's short story collection.**

Get your copy when you sign up to my newsletter today! https://BookHip.com/PBVBNSV